This edition published in 1990 by Gallery Books,
an imprint of W.H. Smith Publishers, Inc.
112 Madison Avenue, New York, New York 10016

Produced for Gallery Books by Joshua Morris Publishing, Inc.,
221 Danbury Road, Wilton, CT 06897

Copyright © 1990 Joshua Morris Publishing, Inc.
All rights reserved. Printed in Hong Kong.
ISBN 0-8317-7254-9

Gallery Books are available for bulk purchase
for sales promotions and premium use.
For details write or telephone the Manager of Special Sales,
W.H. Smith Publishers, Inc., 112 Madison Avenue,
New York, New York 10016   (212) 532-6600.

MOTHER GOOSE
Playtime Rhymes

Illustrated by Robin Lawrie

GALLERY BOOKS
An Imprint of W. H. Smith Publishers Inc.
112 Madison Avenue
New York City 10016

RING A RING O'ROSES

Ring a ring o'roses
A pocket full of posies.
A-tishoo! A-tishoo!
We all fall down.

WEE WILLIE WINKIE

Wee Willie Winkie runs through the town,
Upstairs and downstairs, in his nightgown,
Rapping at the windows, crying through the locks,
"Are all the children in their beds?
Now it's eight o'clock."

SING A SONG OF SIXPENCE

Sing a song of sixpence,
A pocket full of rye,
Four-and-twenty blackbirds
Baked in a pie.

When the pie was opened,
The birds began to sing;
Wasn't that a dainty dish
To set before the King?

TO MARKET

To market, to market, to buy a fat pig,
Home again, home again, jiggety jig.
To market, to market, to buy a fat hog,
Home again, home again, jiggety jog.
To market, to market, to buy a plum bun,
Home again, home again, market is done.

LITTLE JACK HORNER

Little Jack Horner
Sat in a corner
Eating his Christmas pie.
He put in his thumb,
And pulled out a plum,
And said, "What a good boy am I!"

SIMPLE SIMON

Simple Simon met a pieman,
Going to the fair.
Said Simple Simon to the pieman,
"Let me taste your ware."

Said the pieman to Simple Simon,
"Show me first your penny."
Said Simple Simon to the pieman,
"Indeed, I have not any."

Simple Simon went a-fishing
For to catch a whale.
All the water he could find
Was in his mother's pail!

He went for water with a sieve,
But soon it all ran through.
And now poor Simple Simon
Bids you all adieu.

MARY'S LAMB

Mary had a little lamb,
Its fleece was white as snow,
And everywhere that Mary went,
The lamb was sure to go.

It followed her to school one day,
Which was against the rule,
It made the children laugh and play
To see a lamb at school.

POLLY PUT THE KETTLE ON

Polly, put the kettle on,
Polly, put the kettle on,
Polly, put the kettle on,
We'll all have tea.
Sukey, take it off again,
Sukey, take it off again,
Sukey, take it off again,
They've all gone away.

BANBURY CROSS

Ride a cock-horse to Banbury Cross,
To see a fine lady upon a white horse.
With rings on her fingers, and bells on her toes,
She shall have music wherever she goes.

THREE BLIND MICE

Three blind mice; three blind mice.
See how they run! See how they run!
They all ran after the farmer's wife,
Who cut off their tails with a carving knife.
Did you ever see such a sight in your life
As three blind mice?

LITTLE KITTY

I love little Kitty,
Her coat is so warm,
And if I don't hurt her,
She'll do me no harm.

So I'll not pull her tail,
Nor drive her away,
But Kitty and I
Very gently will play.

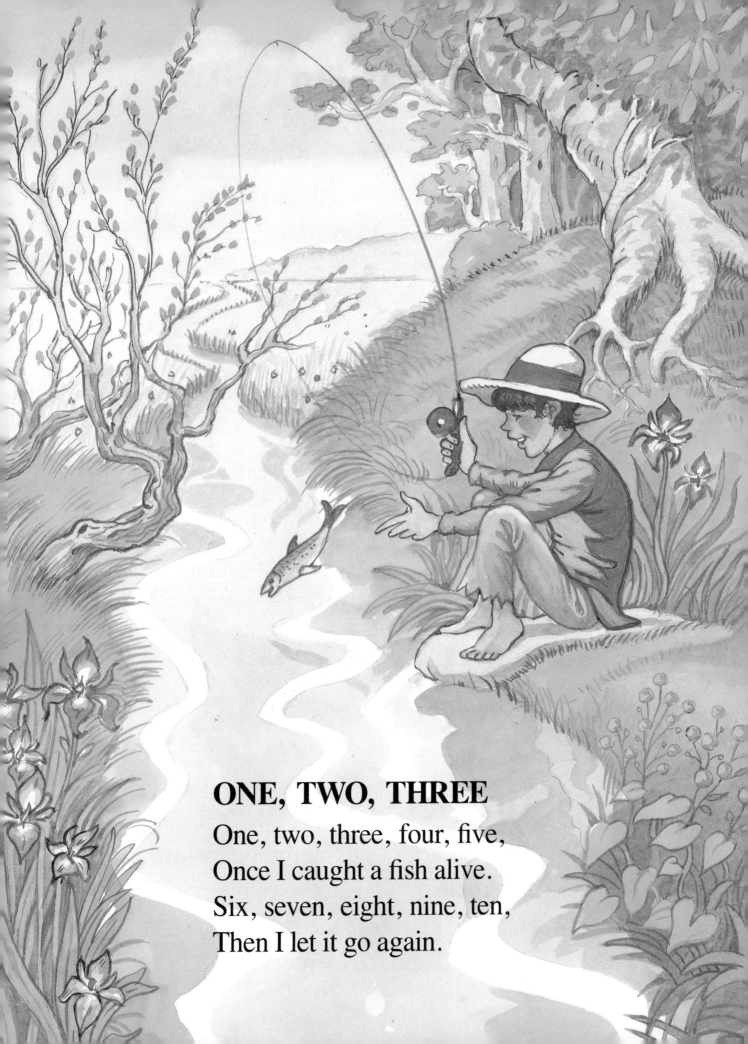

ONE, TWO, THREE

One, two, three, four, five,
Once I caught a fish alive.
Six, seven, eight, nine, ten,
Then I let it go again.

SEE-SAW, MARGERY DAW

See-saw, Margery Daw,
Jacky shall have a new master.
He shall have but a penny a day,
Because he can't work any faster.

THE MULBERRY BUSH

Here we go round the mulberry bush,
The mulberry bush, the mulberry bush.
Here we go round the mulberry bush,
On a cold and frosty morning.

ROCK-A-BYE BABY

Rock-a-bye baby, on the treetop,
When the wind blows, the cradle will rock.
When the bough breaks, the cradle will fall,
And down will come baby, cradle and all.

FIVE TOES

This little pig went to market...

This little pig stayed home...

This little pig had roast beef...

This little pig had none...

And this little pig said, "Wee, wee, wee!"

All the way home.